D1526256

JAMES BRANCH CABELL

By

CARL VAN DOREN

ROBERT M. McBRIDE & COMPANY
NEW YORK :: :: :: :: :: :: 1932

*Printed in the United
States of America*

First Printing, February, 1925
Second Printing, November, 1925
New and Revised Edition,
February, 1932

CONTENTS

James Branch Cabell

I. CABELL MINOR

THERE are more arguments to prove that James Branch Cabell is a legend than to prove that he is a fact. The most dependable of contemporary authorities says of him that he is an "author; *b.* Richmond, Va., Apr. 14, 1879; *s.* Robert Gamble and Anne (Branch) C.; A.B., William and Mary, 1898; *m.* Priscilla, *d.* William Joseph Bradley, of 'Auburn,' Charles City Co., Va., Nov. 8, 1913; 1 son, Ballard Hartwell. Instr. French and Greek, William and Mary, 1896–7; worked in press-room Richmond (Va.) Times, 1898; on staff New York Herald, 1899–1901, and Richmond (Va.) News, 1901; contributor of short stories, etc., to leading mags., 1902–10; was engaged in coal-mining in W. Va., 1911–13; genealogist Va. S. R., 1919–20; historian Va. Soc. Colonial Wars, 1916–29, Va. Soc. S. A. R., 1917–

23; pres. Va. Writers' Club, 1918–21; editor Va. War History Commn., 1919–26; mem. Kappa Alpha (Southern), Phi Beta Kappa. Episcopalian." To these details this most juiceless of contemporary authorities adds only the titles of Mr. Cabell's various books and his address. Remarkably little else about him as a person has been made public: a few attractive but non-committal photographs, a few bits of information little above the level of amiable gossip. All that emerges is the evidence that he is a Virginian of the old stock, cultivated and reticent, who with unvarying fidelity if with varying fortunes has given himself to the writing of books.

The legend which has grown up about Mr. Cabell no doubt owes its exuberance to the scarcity of the facts upon which it has been fed. It babbles, as he has pointed out, about his "romantic irony, his cosmic japes, his bestial obscenities, his well-nigh perfect prose, his soaring imagination, his corroding pessimism," with tiresome reiteration. It speaks largely about his great acquisitions of medieval lore, and hints less largely at his excessive learning in various forbidden topics. It whispers, elsewhere, of such spiritual misdemeanors as in other ages were called compacts with the devil. It goes, even, to the length of mentioning, at a safe distance from the laws concerning libel, misdemeanors not so spiritual. That the legendary aspects of Mr. Cabell, however unwarranted, have such vitality shows well enough that they spring from the rich soil of public ignorance. It may, nevertheless, be admitted that he has enriched the growth by his habits of secrecy and innuendo and mystification and by his obvious disregard of the patterns of thought and sentiment by which his readers naturally expect him to cut his fictions. If he conceals so much, they reason, he must have still more to withhold from the light of day. If he disregards the customary patterns, he must himself regard dark and dangerous ones.

Meanwhile Mr. Cabell, keeping the facts to himself and doubtless smiling at the legend, has gone on in his avowed practice of the desire "to write perfectly of beautiful happenings." And the time has come when it is no longer possible to resist the temptation to examine his aims and his achievements in the long, rich first chapter of his career.

Nor is it easy to resist the temptation to say, at the outset, that Mr. Cabell is already a classic if any American novelist of this century is. The shifts of taste from age to age may now depress and now exalt the credit of the famous *Jurgen*, but so have they done during the past five generations with *Tristram Shandy*, another masterpiece frequently baited by the sort of censor who dreads wit unless it picks its topics with caution. Both by its wit and by its beauty, *Jurgen* is entitled to survive. Moreover, it is far from being its author's only claim to eminence. Certain of his admirers debate among themselves whether *Figures of Earth* is not profounder than *Jurgen*, or *The High Place* more artfully narrated, or *Domnei* lovelier, or *The Silver Stallion* loftier and shrewder. *Chivalry* was a particular favorite of Mark Twain, who kept it at his bedside. And these are but six of the eighteen Cabell volumes which stand closely linked together in the careful scheme according to which they are all arranged. Even though, as is inevitable, two or three of them will outlive the others, the entire eighteen must be taken into account.

There they stand, graceful and compact, devoted to the record of beautiful happenings in a language which never falls below a high level of perfection. They deal with a world which at first may seem extraordinarily remote from the concerns of most recent fiction. That world, however, the invented medieval province of Poictesme, speedily grows familiar to any imagination which ventures into it without undue prejudice, for it has its own logic, as well as its own history and geography. Human life is there as vain a thing as in Ecclesiastes, but it abounds in the dramas of aspiration and desire by which the thread of existence is carried on. Only through the gate of irony, indeed, may this imagined universe be entered. Solemn souls will miss the gate and fumble along an impenetrable wall. But less solemn spirits, passing blithely through the gate, find one of the most exquisite worlds in fiction. It is full of magnificent adventures, high speeches, chivalrous and gallant personages. The landscapes are of agreeable proportions, with smooth lawns and fragrant orchards, with forests and mountains ripe with color. The costumes and the interiors are scrupulously considered, that they may all be beautiful, or at least significant. The cross roads of history meet in this world, and space no less than time comes to a focus there. Yet nothing tawdry or sprawling has been admitted. All is order and art. While there is plenty of satire, it rarely concerns itself with temporary matters. There is learning, but it lays no serious burden upon the stories; there are opinions, but they waste little time in wrangling over controverted issues. Whoever reads these books and comprehends the scheme which now binds them into unity, will feel that Mr. Cabell, like another Adam, has found his Eden, has dressed and tended it, has populated and civilized it, and has made it the home of valor and beauty and wit.

No wonder that, almost thirty years after the appearance of his first book, Mr. Cabell, intrenched behind the uniform edition of his works, looks back with a resentful eye upon the early and scattered volumes which are hunted by collectors and bibliographers as the rarer volumes of no other contemporary American are hunted. Like Holofernes, this iconoclastic Virginian would prefer to hack the Cabell of yesterday merrily into pieces and give him to the Cabell of to-morrow for his breakfast. "Were the choice afforded me," the Holofernian Cabell says, "no one of these first editions . . . would to-day exist." Such iconoclasm, however, cannot be permitted, or at least will not be permitted so long as a single investigator is curious about the steps by which Mr. Cabell, with seldom matched fidelity, has advanced from the region of tentative experiments to the region through which he now manœuvers on surer, more ironic feet. The miracle of his emergence from the world in which he grew up is at once too exciting and too edifying to be forgotten in the stir caused by his arrival in a very different world. Even the most secular scripture need not hesitate to begin with some kind of Genesis.

Concerning the ardent, absurd youth who wrote *The Eagle's Shadow* the Cabell who wrote *Straws and Prayer-Books* speaks disarmingly in a late autobiographic note. "I would like," that youth is made to say, "to write the very nicest sort of books—like Henry

Harland's and Justus Miles Forman's and Anthony Hope's. They would be about beautiful, fine girls and really splendid young men, and everything would come out all right in the end. . . . I simply want to contribute to the best magazines, and write some wholesome . . . entertaining books, that will sell like *The Cardinal's Snuff-Box* and *The Prisoner of Zenda*." In 1902, of course, such aspirations were not entirely quaint. Cloaks and masks were in the mode. Approved heroines waited in Ruritanias or Graustarks for the dashing heroes who should come from England or the United States and rescue them from the thorns by which they were surrounded. The paths of romance led to the greenwood, to the medieval tournament or pleasaunce, to the age of periwig and patch and small sword and furbelow, to the more recent drawing-room or terrace where repartee glittered over tea-tables. *The Eagle's Shadow*, let it be remembered, appeared as a serial in what was shortly to be the most popular of all the popular magazines, and the brief tales by its author which dressed this weightier dish found their way into periodicals of estab-

lished reputation, to be illustrated by established illustrators. There was no serious disregard of current fashion in Mr. Cabell's tender reinterpretations of Falstaff or Villon or in his heartening discovery that the most frivolous beau and belle had really hearts of gold. Few readers of these stories noticed the hand of irony within the glove of velvet.

The hand, nevertheless, inhabited the glove. Mr. Cabell was already in several respects a scholar and a critic. At William and Mary he had taught French and Greek while still an undergraduate; in his first acknowledged contribution to belles-lettres he had taken Congreve for his theme and had defended that insouciant wit against either moralists or apologists. The infection of maturity had commenced to work. "From the start," the latest Cabell was subsequently to warn the earliest, "will be tugging at your pen a pig-headed imp that will be guiding it his way instead of the way you intended. And with each book he will be growing stronger and more importunate and more cunning, and he will be stealing the pen away from you for longer and longer intervals. And by and by that imp, full grown now and the very devil of a taskmaster, will be dictating your books from beginning to end—not to speak here of his making you sweat blood when you revise, at his orders, all the earlier ones. . . . You . . . will call him the desire to write perfectly of beautiful happenings."

The maturer Cabell has so carefully obliterated his tracks, with what looks, at many points, like an amused mendacity, that it is difficult now to guess just when in his career he settled upon the design which has finally come to govern all his material. He himself explains that the inception of his scheme goes back to 1901, "when I wrote the first of the stories bound up together as *The Line of Love.* And the general 'method' followed in that volume—of depicting a decisive event in the lives of two persons, then a similar untying of knots in the life of a child of that couple, and yet afterward in one of the grandchildren's life-history—has been extended, but never altered, in my succeeding volumes. . . . And all traces —pretty clearly now—from Dom Manuel, and the descendants whom he and Alianora left in England, and the other descendants whom he and Niafer left in Poictesme, and from the eleven images that he and Freydis informed with fire from Audela, and set to live as men among mankind." Whenever Mr. Cabell definitely undertook to elaborate his richly colored genealogy, at least he did not, as a careful examination of those anathematized first editions shows, for some time unmistakably reveal his scheme. The unity of his work lay in his temper, in his comparative disinclination, or inability, to invent, in the gradual drift of his imagination toward two or three settings and two or three sets of characters for which eventually he gave up all others. While this unity was asserting itself, he moved about through medieval France and eighteenth-century England and contemporary America, searching for episodes worthy to be recounted in his tone of mingled rapture and skepticism.

The episodes in his volumes of short stories, *The Line of Love*, *Gallantry*, *Chivalry*, *The Certain Hour*, are essentially gestures. With poets and warriors as their almost invariable heroes, and love as their almost invariable theme, they set forth each of them some high moment of valor or renunciation in which much is demanded of the hero, who meets it with even more than is demanded. François Villon, in *In Necessity's Mortar*, for the last time sees Catherine de Vaucelles, who has jilted him and shamed him, discovers that she still loves him, but, now that through years of despair he has become a mere "hog with a voice," decides that he must kill her love to save her, and so disavows any preference for her whatever. The Prince de Gâtinais, in *The Scapegoats*, having with one dire gesture poisoned his son's low-born sweetheart to give the younger man to his high-born duty and to France, with another tremendous gesture poisons himself in expiation for a deed which he does not in the least regret. At such moments the protagonists of this universe rise above the customary stature of mankind, touching the cold stars with heads full of mad, glorious conceits. Mr. Cabell knows that the gestures are for the most part vain. Villon, crying out in agony over his obligation, finds that his cry suggests a neat ballade. "So, dismissing for the while his misery, he fell to considering, with undried cheeks, what rhymes he needed." Louis de Soyecourt, by his father's action made Duke of Noumaria, in the end escapes from the boredom of his duty to a happy vagabondage as a piano-tuner. Yet though the conceits are mad, they are glorious. Who would live forever? Who would take love at less than the peak and then, through dwindling years, have nothing supernal to remember? Who would miss the chance once in a lifetime to confound all foes and rivals with a magnanimity which though bitter must seem immense? Mr. Cabell has a weakness for these gestures that gives him, as an artist, strength.

The danger which has always hung over Mr. Cabell in his chronicling of such gestures is the danger of sentimentalism. Lovely as a bubble may be, it can be broken by one puff too much, and then nothing is left of its iridescence. The puff too much he occasionally gave in his earlier versions. As *The Housewife*, for instance, at present stands, King Edward is content to speak thus of his queen when he hears of her great loyalty: "She waddles. . . . Still, I am blessed." But once the passage ran more loftily: "Now at last he understood the heart of Philippa. 'Let me live,' the king prayed; 'O Eternal Father, let me live

a little while that I may make atonement!'"
There was a time, that is to say, when Mr. Cabell blurred the fine edge of his rapture by moments of passion wherein he forgot to be sophisticated. Verbal changes here and there in the revision have been necessary to cut away an earlier softness, particularly when his warriors tended to be poets or orators at dramatic crises. This difficulty does not arise when his heroes are technically poets, as they are in *The Certain Hour*. Of them it may reasonably be expected that they will bear themselves with a zest and wit which would hardly be allowed them, even at the most striking turns of their careers, were they men of some more prosaic calling and language. But then Mr. Cabell's heroes are all actually, in one degree or another, poets, much like those young men who lift and enliven the plays of Shakspere. Again and again the Cabellian theme is the conflict between a poet and a warrior for the same lady; and though the poet as a rule has the neater tongue and the quicker intelligence, he has no marked advantage over his rival in goldenness of speech. The poets are warriors and the warriors are poets. To keep such

equations credible, Mr. Cabell has been obliged to lay his scenes ordinarily in ages which cherished both valor and poetry and which held them interwoven with delicate codes of honor. With one of his favored ages he associates the cult of Chivalry; with the other, Gallantry.

"The cornerstone of Chivalry I take to be the idea of vicarship: for the chivalrous person is, in his own eyes at least, the child of God, and goes about this world as his Father's representative in an alien country. It was very adroitly to human pride, through an assumption of man's responsibility in his tiniest action, that Chivalry made its appeal; and exhorted every man to keep faith, not merely with the arbitrary will of a strong god, but with himself. There is no cause for wonder that the appeal was irresistible, when to each man it thus admitted that he himself was the one thing seriously to be considered. . . . So man became a chivalrous animal; and about this flattering notion of divine vicarship builded his elaborate medieval code, to which, in essentials, a great number of persons adhere even nowadays." Had Mr. Cabell been less a poet himself, he might have fallen into astringency with such a conception as his starting-point. As it is, the conception merely furnishes the ironic edge which shears away the exuberance to which his love of gestures might have led him. He does not, on account of this comic attitude, take less interest in the chivalrous impulses which his characters exhibit. Bound by their sense of responsibility to an extent which he knows is comic, they yet conduct themselves with a high seriousness which, while it lasts, is the breeder of superb rhetoric and noble actions, and incidentally of admirable drama. Each of them, man or woman, in *Chivalry* and in the allied stories of the other volumes, is ringed round with perils, and each of them bears himself magnificently to the point of death or whatever different reward awaits him.

Mr. Cabell's Gallantry is enough like his Chivalry in its consequences to those who live by it. "Now the essence of Gallantry, I take it, was to accept the pleasures of life leisurely and its inconveniences with a shrug. . . . A gallant person will . . . always bear in mind that in love-affairs success is less the Ultima

Thule of desire than its *coup de grâce*, and he will be careful never to admit the fact, especially to himself. . . . He will prink; and he will be at his best after sunset. He will dare . . . to acknowledge the shapeliness of a thief's leg; to concede that the commission of murder does not necessarily impair the agreeableness of the assassin's conversation; and to insist that . . . God is kindlier than the genteel would regard as rational. He will, in fine, sin on sufficient provocation, and repent within the moment, quite sincerely, and be not unconscionably surprised when he repeats the progression. And he will consider the world with a smile of toleration, and his own doings . . . with a smile of honest amusement, and Heaven with a smile that is not distrustful." Gallantry, indeed, is a sort of frivolous Chivalry, living up to its code on a plane of life where less seems to be involved in the issue of any given event than on the plane of vicarship. But there is for all that a rapier in every ruffled hand which is celebrated in *Gallantry*. John Bulmer, Duke of Ormskirk, protagonist of *In the Second April*, is the quintessential Cabell hero of the earlier books. Like all his fellows, he reflects often upon the boy he used to be and makes much of an old love, but he knows that he does not too violently regret his past nor too poignantly remember the Alison of his first April. Now seasoned in the world, he matches and over-matches it with a cunning which he cannot forego even in his courtship of Claire de Puysange. He distresses her, who is less than half his age, with his persistent lightness on the most desperate occasions, yet at their great occasion he meets his enemies with a courage as unassailable as if he did not accompany it with words of such laughing eloquence as madden her before they convince her. Bulmer cuts the figure that every quick-spirited youth and every full-hearted man would like to cut. He is, to be sure, a dream of gallant perfection, and no more; but he curiously stirs the blood of man and boy alike. And with what art Mr. Cabell constructs the drama of Bulmer's wooing and winning: the incognito sustained yet recognized, the rejection endured with pain yet with gay fortitude, the magnificent duel on the tower! It is, perhaps, the art of Congreve, but of a Congreve warmed with rich colors and a generous audacity.

In the towered cathedral which Mr. Cabell has gradually built, on the level plain of current life, for his undeviating worship of beauty and heroism, the short stories of these four volumes are the smaller chapels braced against the central structure, the ornaments carved boldly on the weather side or tucked away in shadowy corners to tempt the curious. Without, it should be made clear, unparalleled erudition, he has nevertheless ransacked many remote places for his materials and his patterns. His universe in various fashions resembles that of *The Faërie Queene*, wherein geographical and chronological boundaries melt and flow, wherein fable encroaches upon history, and the creative mood of the poet re-cuts his shining fabrics as if they were whole cloth intended solely for his purposes. Mr. Cabell has a partiality for the Middle Ages, when the fates of the European nations were tangled with contending dynasties, and for the eighteenth century, but, like Spenser, he draws upon the ancient world and the world of dreams. In choosing those dramatic moments which he has elected to record, he tends to choose occasions about which history is partly silent in the lives of its eminent men and women: a late meeting of Falstaff with a boyhood sweetheart, the forced decision of Villon to turn thief, the final interview of Marlowe with the girl he loves, the apocryphal courtship of Katharine of Valois and Henry V, the philosophical plagiarism of Shakspere in writing *The Tempest*, the mysterious death of Herrick, the marriage of Wycherley to the Countess of Drogheda and of Sheridan to Miss Ogle. Not that Mr. Cabell is confined to history, even thus lightly handled; he has no objection to inventing poets and warriors when he needs them, nor to being as circumstantial about them as about the genuine personages of his tales. But he requires the added glamour which is given to fiction by its association with remembered or rumored facts. Beautiful happenings, he knows, seem more beautiful when they have already been looked upon as memorable.

The temper with which he approaches all these themes has from the first been ironic, so much so that he regularly distresses readers who prefer to have their romances entirely romantic. His heroes are not forever heroes.

The tide turns with them, and the sun sets, and the flower fades. Perhaps he early learned to glory in his disillusionment; at least he has never relaxed into credulity. Consequently he does not tell his stories with an abandoned rush of narrative. They move on deliberate feet, their episodes rounded out with a steady-handed art. Always Mr. Cabell interprets the action in the terms of a spectator who knows that though ecstasy is supreme it is also vain. At the same time, there is that in his constitution which will not let him merely strip and dissect. He must adorn while he analyzes.

To this element is due his other essential quality as a story-teller, his silken texture. There are no angles in his surfaces. His style purrs to a degree that now and then begets monotony; his phrases, ordinarily so felicitous, now and then have a mannered look; he so often avoids the simple way of saying simple things that he overloads his language. It is hard to remember his plots, less hard to remember his characters, because they have been hidden under his suave tapestry. At his best, however, and he is very frequently at his best in his short stories, he is crystal in his meanings and delicately varied in his rhythms, as in this speech credited to Shakspere: "Lord, what a deal of ruined life it takes to make a little art! Yes, yes, I know. Under old oaks lovers will mouth my verses, and the acorns are not yet shaped from which those oaks will spring. My adoration and your perfidy, all that I have suffered, all that I have failed in even, has gone toward the building of an enduring monument. All these will be immortal, because youth is immortal, and youth delights in demanding explanations of infinity. And only to this end I have suffered and have catalogued the ravings of a perverse disease which has robbed my life of all the normal privileges of life as flame shrivels hair from the arm—that young fools such as I was once might be pleased to murder my rhetoric, and scribblers parody me in their fictions, and schoolboys guess at the date of my death!" Had Mr. Cabell no other gift than to make wisdom thus descant upon the vanity of life, his most persistent and successful theme, he would still deserve a praise as worthy as he is likely to receive in a world which his Shakspere all too accurately describes.

With the short stories which are as chapels to the Cabellian cathedral must be ranked the five novels which have their scenes in or near or not too far from Lichfield and Fairhaven, those romantic cities which the world thinks of as Virginian, though Mr. Cabell softly points out that he has never asserted as much. They are pleasant cities, contentedly provincial, where the codes of Chivalry and Gallantry persist with something of the old colors under no matter how changed conditions. If these cities embrace within their habits such necessities as labor or such luxuries as prayer, little mention is made of them. Their business, so far as the novels are concerned, is love—love made with eloquent words and with delicate codes of honor. A few men do most of the love-making: Gerald Musgrave, Felix Kennaston, Robert Etheridge Townsend, Rudolph Musgrave, John Charteris. Their careers run through *Something About Eve*, *The Eagle's Shadow*, *The Cords of Vanity*, *The Rivet in Grandfather's Neck*, *The Cream of the Jest* like the cheerful warp of many varied textures. This or that man of them may have some tender loyalty to his first love, and may often brood over it with edifying sentiments, but for the most part they move among the exquisite, glimmering girls of Lichfield and Fairhaven like the heroes of Restoration comedy, touching a hand here, taking a kiss there, breaking hearts and themselves becoming heart-broken, recovering, as do their ladies, with the long sighs of the sentimental and with the light hearts of the heroic. It is the women who make the texture varied. There are, indeed, not as many of them as might be expected in five novels, for they, no less than the men, may reappear in this or that new plot when they have finished their courses in another. But they have such diversity in themselves that the stories are rich with their changing moods. To love one of these women is a kind of polygamy. Neither Mr. Cabell nor the lover of any of them studies her deeply enough to strike into the regions where biology holds the lantern, and where all women, it is argued, are alike. The ladies of Lichfield and Fairhaven are the ladies of high comedy. Not shallow, they are gay; not solemn, they are intelligent. They are the decorative elements which give a charming surface to records of love conceived cynically yet tenderly.

The records themselves range from such a less than characteristic story as that in *The Eagle's Shadow*, with its sillabub dialogues and its theatrical solution, to such a more than characteristic story as that in *The Cream of the Jest*, with its two universes always suspended in the hand of the narrator and turned, now the one, now the other, uppermost, and on to *Something About Eve*, which is in a sense an antidote to all the others. Perhaps none of the plots, except that of *The Eagle's Shadow*, is less than characteristic of its author in his maturity. What stretches out through *The Cords of Vanity* is merely another line of love, with a single personage serving as the lover in all cases. Robert Etheridge Townsend, poet and romancer, ascends to peak after peak of rapture, rejoices there with the enchanting mistress of the hour, and then slips down again to the ironical valley of his daily life, which knows that the magic of love is only a brief madness. He is a sorry fellow, deft with words and fickle with emotions. So are Charteris and Kennaston, only one of them permitted a novel to himself in this series, but neither of them ever far from any chapter. By their recurrence they make clear that the method of the Lichfield-Fairhaven novels is not essentially different from that of the books of short stories. Whether short or long, the narratives are all episodes, in sequence or distinct, little dramas given over to exposing the vanity of human pretensions and human desires. A few situations, adroitly varied, Mr. Cabell finds enough for his purposes; and he would rather bring an old, successful character back upon the stage than go to the trouble of shaping a new, untried one. Moreover, he wants his heroes to comprehend as well as to endure their fates. Not for him the blind tragedy and the dumb victim. His lovers burn as other lovers do, but his lovers even at the summit of felicity are aware of what is passing, and after due sufferings they heal themselves with the unembittered smile which is the light of comedy. So exigent with regard to his characters and their attitudes toward their adventures, Mr. Cabell is bound to be confined to a few settings, a few actions, a few personages. His variety lies in the by-paths by which so many of his plots are conducted to virtually the same end and in the luster of the language which with so many surprising graces fits itself to nearly the same theme.

The theme, nevertheless, now and then reaches out to touch aspects of existence which do not properly belong within its narrower bounds. *The Rivet in Grandfather's Neck*, for example, has for its chief personage the gallant genealogist Rudolph Musgrave, of the Musgraves of Matocton, who, through all the wonder of his love for the girl who marries him, cherishes the memory of the girl who married Charteris instead and whom Musgrave has protected from a disillusioning knowledge of her husband by one more heroic gesture. Yet the *Rivet* is also an edged and beguiling satire. Musgrave, that quaint figure whittled out of chivalry and dressed up in amiable heroics, is a Southern gentleman comically perceived and rendered; the narrative glances obliquely at all the follies and affectations and absurdities of the traditional South. Gerald Musgrave in *Something About Eve*, though he leaves his natural body working industriously in Lichfield and himself lives elsewhere on Mispec

Moor with Maya, is the most domesticated of the Cabell heroes. However remote and various his adventures may be, they lead him only to old conclusions. Enough a poet to undertake his long-foiled journey toward Antan, he is too much a man not to come back convinced that homely ways are, for him, better. Felix Kennaston in *The Cream of the Jest* balances the hemispheres of his experience. He lives in comfortable Lichfield much as its more representative citizens live there, but in the excursions of his imagination he visits that world which, by never having existed, partly atones to men for the world that does exist. These two universes are not separated in *The Cream of the Jest* by any tight wall which it is a strain to jump over; they flow with witching caprice one into another, affording endless opportunities to compare the universe in which Kennaston lives as Kennaston with the universe in which he lives as Horvendile. In a sense, his career is an allegory with the human race for its larger hero. Does not the race, unable to endure the pain or boredom of its earth, turn perennially to the clouds and skies and create better regions to dream in? Is the experience actually more real than the vision? Clearly it may be argued, as indeed it is argued by Felix Kennaston, that men and women are nothing more than characters in the mystifying plot which some great Romancer is weaving over their heads. They travel ordinarily at the pedestrian gait which among them is called realism when they imitate it in their own works of art; but now and then they are lifted and driven by incalculable urges which are perhaps the lyric or dramatic moments in the life of the Romancer who has created them.

Some such idea lies back of all that Mr. Cabell has written. It is, of course, the basis of his argument for romance, and it serves to furnish his narratives, short or long, with their rich color and high, ironic language. The idea in him is so persistent that it might make him, in his unconcern with the surface activities of men, a languid story-teller if he did not have an amount of comic vigor which is sometimes overlooked in the delight his language and color give. It might make him, also, more monotonous in his disillusion than he is, thanks to the gusto with which he savors the phantasmagoric spectacle of human life.

But thus at once detached and avid, he has been able to practise his art with the disinterested scruples which set the general level of his excellence above that of any other contemporary American novelist. Nevertheless, there is a major and there is a minor Cabell. To the second must be ascribed the short stories, though some of them are masterpieces within their limits, for the sole reason that they are, as episodes, unable to display their author's larger qualities at the full. To the minor Cabell, not much less surely, belong the Lichfield-Fairhaven chronicles, by reason of a certain slightness in their substance and a certain remoteness from that Poictesme which Mr. Cabell has come, like Felix Kennaston, to inhabit more naturally, and perhaps more really, than any tangible province.

II. CABELL MAJOR

THE Poictesme which Mr. Cabell has created and gradually populated with a whole dynasty and its subjects, friends, and enemies, lies somewhere on the map of Europe —nearer Provence, no doubt, than Poictiers or Angoulesme. The country was a fief of the wicked King Ferdinand of Castile and Léon, who beheaded his old friend the rightful count, to make a place for Manuel. At that time, which was 1234, Poictesme was in the hands of the Northmen under Duke Asmund, later expelled. Not too far from Provence, neither was it too far from Scotland, both of which Manuel visited on his way to claim his new possession. It had a sea-coast, the cities of Bellegarde and Storisende in which Manuel ordinarily lived, and many dark woods and twilight heaths and haunted mountains. It engaged in diplomatic relations with France and England, to say nothing of less formal contacts between its rulers and all the countries, real or imagined, of the medieval universe. Scandinavia poetically impinged upon the province, with Constantinople and Barbary, Massilia, Aquitaine, Navarre, Portugal, Rome, Alexandria, Arcadia, Olympus, Asgard, and the Jerusalems Old and New. Though it seems to have seen its great days in the thirteenth century, it was still prosperous as late as the eighteenth. Nothing, indeed, in the matter of geography or history is impossible to Poictesme, for it is, of course, a pure creation. Mr. Cabell may please himself with skirting actuality in a hundred or a thousand details, as he does; but his innumerable elusions are only incidental to a deliberate scheme. Having found no world in which he could be satisfied to build the structure of his art, he has invented and completed one.

Because he has been in one of his professions a genealogist, Mr. Cabell sees Poictesme with something of the genealogist's eye. Manuel, Count and Redeemer of the province, is also its prime ancestor. From his heroic loins spring all the later Cabellian generations, whether in Poictesme or out of it. By Niafer he is the father of the Melicent of *Domnei*, the

Dorothy la Désirée of *Jurgen*, the Ettarre of *The Cream of the Jest*, as well as of the Emmerick who succeeds him; this line reaches, by way of the short stories, down through the English Allonbys and Bulmers to the American Rudolph Musgrave and Felix Kennaston and Robert Etheridge Townsend of *The Cords of Vanity* and *The Rivet in Grandfather's Neck*. By Alianora of Provence, technically wife of Henry III of England, Manuel is the father of Edward I, whose descendants are numerous and impressive. In a different fashion Manuel has the help of Freydis in the process of informing with almost human fire the ten figures which he has modeled and which move among mankind as the poets of *The Certain Hour*, wherein Shakspere and Herrick and Wycherley and Pope and Sheridan are brothers in clay of the John Charteris who is Mr. Cabell's mouthpiece in *Beyond Life*. Moreover, the skein of all these lines of descent is tangled. The blood of Manuel touches that of the lords of Puysange, so famous in Poictesme and in so many Cabell stories; Edward Longshanks is reprehensibly related to the Bulmers; Cynthia Allonby appears as the

Dark Lady of Shakspere. Even though Mr. Cabell has in his later books, and in the later editions of his earlier books, laid an increasing emphasis upon the genealogical unity of his characters, he from the first worked in a manner which made it possible for him thus to draw them together when he was ready.

This unity in Poictesme has thrown into a higher and higher relief the two great figures who dominate it, not only because they are eminent in that country but because they between them manage to exhibit virtually all the human qualities which interest Mr. Cabell. They are Manuel the Redeemer and Jurgen the pawnbroker. Characteristically, their creator refers to what he calls his original sources, *Les Gestes de Manuel* and *La Haulte Histoire de Jurgen*, and he unearths a literary historian to say for him that: "the Gestes are mundane stories, the History is a cosmic affair, in that, where Manuel faces the world, Jurgen considers the universe. . . . Dom Manuel is the Achilles of Poictesme, as Jurgen is its Ulysses." In his own person Mr. Cabell goes on to say: "Now, roughly, the distinction serves. Yet minute consideration discovers, I think, in these two sets of legends a more profound, if subtler, difference, in the handling of the protagonist: with Jurgen all of the physical and mental man is rendered as a matter of course; whereas in dealing with Manuel there is, always, I believe, a certain perceptible and strange, if not inexplicable, aloofness. Manuel did thus and thus, Manuel said so and so, these legends recount: yes, but never anywhere have I detected any firm assertion as to Manuel's thoughts and emotions, nor any peep into the workings of this hero's mind. . . . These old poets of Poictesme would seem, whether of intention or no, to have dealt with their national hero as an admirable person whom they have never been able altogether to love, or entirely to sympathize with, or to view quite without distrust." Mr. Cabell hints that this may be due to "the natural inability of a poet to understand a man who succeeds in everything," but he himself avers that he is content to follow the old romancers, pointing out that "in real life . . . such is the fashion in which we are compelled to deal with all happenings and with all our fellows, whether they wear or lack the gaudy name of heroism."

Thus cryptically Mr. Cabell suggests that in *Figures of Earth,* his novel devoted to Manuel, he has set himself to portray a man of action busy with his diverse affairs. Manuel, it is true, is essentially an artist. What seems to him his greatest aim is to mold out of clay, in the manner of the gods, certain figures in his own image. But the burden of necessity constantly interrupts him. He is obliged to turn aside from these concerns to redeem and rule Poictesme, to love various women, and to bear himself among men as becomes a hero of his station. Or rather, he permits himself so to be obliged. When he appears upon the scene he is a swineherd in the mythical regions of Rathgor and Lower Targamon. With Suskind, a fairy mistress uncorrupted by sin or salvation, he has studied "the secret of preserving that dissatisfaction which is divine where all else falls away with age into the acquiescence of beasts." Suskind, however, Manuel deserts because he is tempted by the prospects of human glory. At first he is confident enough to take for his motto: "I

follow after my own thinking and my own desires." But among mankind he finds that success is to be purchased at another price, and that the world is eager to be deceived, so he changes his motto to *Mundus vult decipi.* Though at his voice all spells are broken and at his touch all walls tumble down, he is steadily subdued to the color of the universe he lives in. It costs him thirty years to win back Niafer, whom once in his arrogance he had allowed Grandfather Death to take rather than Manuel, but who turns out to be much like any other wife. Having been made Count of Poictesme for no particular reason of his own, he wastes enormous energies in redeeming it, and then is bored by the duties thereby brought upon him. Of the figures which he has, with the unearthly assistance of Queen Freydis, informed with fire, the one which Manuel most values is Sesphra, whose name, after all, is but Phrases transposed. Eventually, this hero with the proud heart spends most of his days in the Room of Ageus, which is an anagram for Usage. Tempted by Suskind to return to her high-hearted garden, he pleads an excuse in his daughter Melicent, though the child actually wearies him whenever he has played with her a quarter of an hour; and when he perceives the insidious mark of Suskind upon Melicent, he goes out and slays the lovely spirit, "whose heart and life was April, and who plotted courageously against the orderings of unimaginative gods." Thereafter it required Grandfather Death to fetch Manuel back to the dim pool of Haranton, where still awaited him the figure of himself which he had long ago begun and never finished.

"Oh, certainly," says Manuel to Grandfather Death, "Count Manuel's achievements were notable and such as were not known anywhere before, and men will talk of them for a long while. Yet, looking back,—now that this famed Count of Poictesme means less to me,—why, I seem to see only the strivings of an ape reft of his tail, and grown rusty at climbing, who has reeled blunderingly from mystery to mystery, with pathetic makeshifts, not understanding anything, greedy in all desires, and always honeycombed with poltroonery. So in a secret place his youth was put away in exchange for a prize that was hardly worth the having;

and the fine geas [bond or obligation] which his mother laid upon him was exchanged for the common geas of what seems expected." This, in half a paragraph, is Mr. Cabell's allegory of worldly success. Through the career of such a demi-demon as Manuel runs the enlarging thread of defeat; the other side of all his triumphs wears the face of loss. Hope falters and courage compromises. The mightiest champion is no better off than Gulliver when he wakes in Lilliput and finds himself bound by countless threads in one helpless position. And the mightiest champion is likely to be worse off, for the chances are that he will accept his threads and by and by make virtues of them.

Thus in *Figures of Earth*, which is called A Comedy of Appearances, the ordinary formula of comedy is reversed. To most ironic commentators it seems amusing that duped boys should cling to visions instead of adjusting themselves with a minimum of conflict to the solid, prudent realities. No story, to such commentators, seems so salutary, and none is employed by them so frequently, as the story of a youth who unlearns unwisdom in the school of secular experience, arriving, at the end, at the conclusion that as the common is the sensible, it is no doubt also the excellent. Though Mr. Cabell is ironic enough, he does not find undeniable doctrine taught in the secular schools. The dreams of youth come back to haunt the wisest men, who may have to admit that the dreams are of a more persistent substance than the daily phantasms which they have pursued. The average millions, who have had no such dreams or who have been so disloyal to them that they remember them only as fumblings in the dark, exult at the spectacle of a hero deprived gradually of the use of his bright wings and harnessed to the customary furrow. This exultation Mr. Cabell challenges. What to him appears comic in the situation is not that the youth should have resisted the world so long but that he should have been taken in by it so completely. The surrender would be tragic were it not shared by so many men and by them so stoutly rationalized into victory. For such rationalizing Mr. Cabell in *Figures of Earth* reserves his chief laughter. As another might laugh at the promises of Suskind, he laughs at the homely counsels of Niafer.

For the center of genuine existence does not in his apprehension coincide with the center of busy mediocrity. He is of another country. In that other country the rapture of love endures without subsiding into comfortable friendship, and glory is measured by a sense of aims perfectly achieved rather than by the buzz of imbecile applause from trivial onlookers. How preposterous that Manuel should have emigrated from such a region to be a commonplace husband and count and father!

Yet there is, Mr. Cabell knows, an argument which goes still further. If the career of Manuel is centripetal, drawing him into the terrestrial vortex, the career of Jurgen is centrifugal, flinging him off through white space and parti-colored time; and the end of both careers is equally age and decrepitude and the sense of universal vanity. For all men live, whatever their rebellions, under the rule of Koshchei the Deathless, who made things as they are. From that rule even the incredible adventures of the pawnbroker of Poictesme cannot free him. Jurgen, having spoken kindly of things as they are, is for a reward permitted to have a year of youth and to move about in the world with his old head upon his young shoulders, an impish, inquisitive, amorous Faust. *Jurgen* is called A Comedy of Justice, but the thing its hero seeks is really what is known as poetic justice because it nowhere exists in the mechanical realm of Koshchei. Nonchalantly during this replevined year Jurgen assumes the titles one after the other of duke and prince and king and emperor and pope. As emperor he ventures into hell; as pope he ascends to heaven, where he seats himself impudently upon the very throne of God. The year takes him to the court where Guenevere is a princess, in that flush of loveliness which had not yet become the flower eventually to seem divine to the knights of Arthur; and Jurgen has the love of Guenevere. The year takes him to Cocaigne, where the only law is that every man shall do that which seems good to him, and where Queen Anaïtis, more often known as the Lady of the Lake, instructs him in many perverse and curious arts; and Jurgen has the love of Anaïtis. The year takes him to Pseudopolis, where Grecian Helen lives married to Achilles and warred upon by

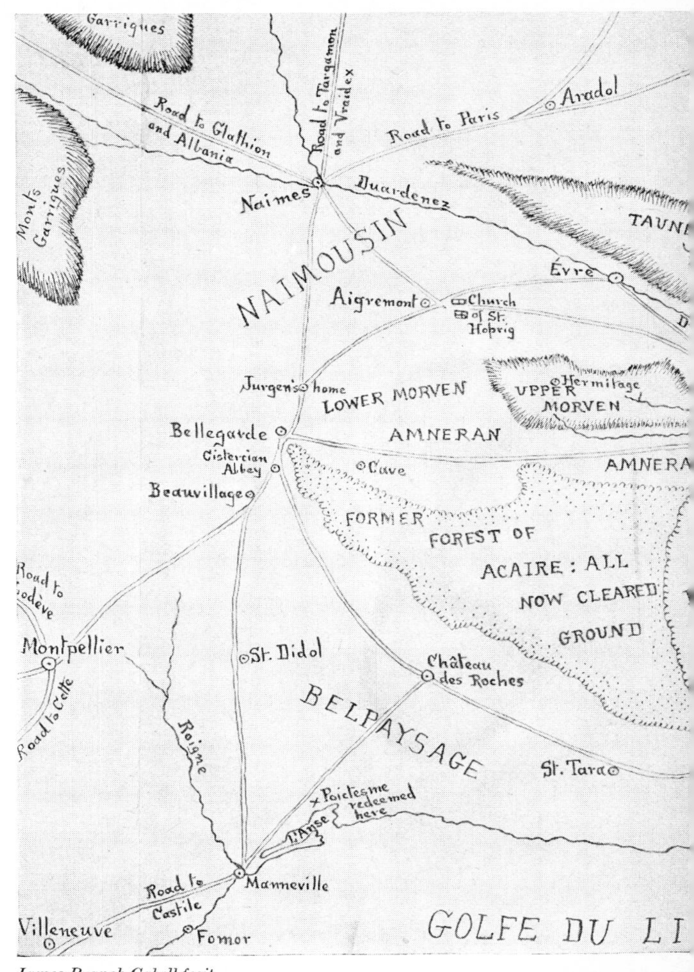

James Branch Cabell fecit

Copied from the frontispiece of: POPULAR TALES OF POICTESME/Supernatural, Romantic and/Legendary/Collected and Illustrated/by John Frederick Lewistam/ (*drawing*)/London:/Sampson Howe, Son, and Marsden,/24, Ludgate Hill./1855./ The Right of Translation is reserved./

This map, be it noted, omits the Bas-Taunenois region (Val-Ardray), which in the thirteenth century formed the northern and eastern frontier of Poictesme. In Val-Ardray were the old Forest of Bovion (now, like a great part of Acaire, cleared ground) and the plains of the Ardre River, then defended (as is shown) by Aradol and, further east, by the fortresses of Nointel, Basardra, Yair and Upper Ardra.

This district would appear to have been, somewhat naïvely, left out by Lewistam so as to make room for his map's title. A similar awkwardness in cartographic art has, one deduces, led to the omission of Lorcha, so often mentioned in the text of the Popular Tales,—that evil tower which stood, of course, in Acaire, about midway between Asch and the Château des Roches. It is noteworthy, for the rest, that this map retains the old name Beauvillage for the little town more ambitiously entitled, since the seventeenth century, Beauséant. Bülg, doubtless, is followed here.

John Bulmer's marriage in the former Forest of Acaire, it is estimated, took place near this map's M in the word "FORMER."

hosts of Philistia; and Jurgen, though too prudent to touch her incomparable beauty and thus bring it into comparison with all the beauty he has tasted, is lifted to a fresh vision of the marvels he had long ago perceived in Dorothy la Désirée, Count Manuel's daughter, whom he loved when he was twenty and a poet. But when, at the end of his great journey, he is offered by Koshchei his choice of these bright women, he sorrowfully rejects all of them. Through knowledge he has lost the code of Chivalry which could have made him suspect divinity in Guenevere; through becoming forty he has lost the zest of the senses which could have made him fix all his desire upon Anaïtis; through infidelity to his old vision of perfection he has lost the courage which might have made him willing to mate with Helen. Though Koshchei with one hand has made him generous offers, Koshchei with the other hand has beaten him. Jurgen finally from too much sugar turns back to honest salt and rejoins his commonplace but comfortable wife.

This much, however, Jurgen owes to the author of *Figures of Earth*: he believes that in thus admitting his tether he has sustained defeat, not gained a victory. "I have become again a creature of use and wont; I am the lackey of prudence and half-measures; and I have put my dreams upon an allowance. . . . I have failed my vision! . . . I have failed, and I know very well that every man must fail: and yet my shame is no less bitter. For I am transmuted by time's handling! I shudder at the thought of living day-in and day-out with my vision. . . . It does not seem fair, but there is no help for it." The justice which Jurgen has hunted through the universe is as much an illusion as the success which Manuel captured. The day comes when the incorrigible dreamer, long cured of his phantasms of reality, suddenly discovers that he has not sufficient faith in anything, not even in his own deductions, and that he must go back to earth as naked as he was when he came out of his mother's womb.

Though the conclusion of *Jurgen* is disillusion, the book itself is a continual delight. The rage of a few zealots has directed attention to certain phallic passages in the narrative, but these so admirably fit the general scheme that only the nimble-snouted root them out and mumble them. For Mr. Cabell, alone among American novelists, the hot writhings and grotesque abandonments of love are as much a part of love's comedy as the more spiritual perturbations, and he has allowed his irony to play over the body hardly less than over the soul of Jurgen. But the real concern of the uproarious legend is with the voyaging, trafficking soul. Such insolence as Jurgen's thrusts itself into every forbidden corner and such intelligence as his brings away at least a little wisdom. These are the territories of romance which he is visiting, wherein the world's imagination has localized the great deeds and emotions which the race remembers; but Jurgen, with his cheeky shrewdness, finds nonsense behind many of the emotions and postures behind many of the deeds. Even in hell there are delusions, for the witty and profound devils who inhabit it are kept busy inventing and executing the torments which men, in the pride of their sins, demand. Indeed, all hell is nothing but an illusion which Koshchei has created for the gratification of vain mankind. Heaven itself, cut by Koshchei on the garish pattern furnished him by Revelations, is another illusion, in which Jurgen's grandmother lives tenderly nourished upon the blisses which she had expected to find there. And how rollickingly on page after page are ridiculed the prudes of Philistia and the excessive claims of democracy, which is the form of government chosen by the devils, and the pretensions of many orthodoxies and the blindness of sentimentalists and the brevity and unreality of appearances. Jurgen looks in turn at all the bubbles of existence, past or present, and pricks them one by one. At the same time, his story is not a continuous snarling. It is full-bodied, a progression full of beauty and pity and mirth, as if a huge organ should burst into laughter.

It is the symbolism of *Jurgen* and *Figures of Earth* which makes them at some points difficult. Mr. Cabell is the most humorous of mythologists. Out of what might seem pedantry if there were less gusto in it, or ignorance if there were less method, he has inextricably jumbled all the mythologies as well as all the histories and geographies. Nor has he hesitated to invent with a large hand. The result is that he crowds his pages with symbols which may be brilliantly suggestive and which may be merely mystification. And mystification, of course, is often irritation. But Mr. Cabell no more minds irritating than he minds mystifying. He works under cover, always by the method of indirection. Not even in a certain priceless copy of *Jurgen* which he once fully annotated for a friend does he give away all his secret meanings. Allegory lurks where no one has any reason to suspect it; allegory is also sometimes absent from passages wherein by all precedent it ought to be. What reader, in such circumstances, can be quite sure that Mr. Cabell is not having sport with him? No one can be sure, and from the uncertainty springs discomfort in downright bosoms. For downright bosoms this comic poet did not write these books. He writes for scholars who are erudite enough to catch a reasonable share of his allusions but not so literal as to be vexed when an allusion goes over their heads; for worldlings who are sophisticated enough to laugh with him at all follies and yet to take no offense if he hints that perhaps even sophistication may be another folly; for poets who are whole enough to follow him to the moon for visions and still to take pleasure with him when he returns to move gleefully about the earth. All told, these scholars and worldlings and poets make up perhaps a smallish audience. That, however, Mr. Cabell knows perfectly. He understands that it is but an illusion of comic justice to hold that good plays are always performed before good houses.

The Manuel and Jurgen sagas are too rich to be exhausted within the limits of a single book apiece. Manuel only disappears from Poictesme, not dies, and so lives on there in deathless prosperity and influence. *The Silver Stallion* is an ironic, poetic chronicle of the stages by which a reputation advances to a cult. The process is no slipshod accident. Jurgen, still a child, has a hand in it. During a truant night, he tells his inquisitorial parents, he saw Manuel transfigured and elevated into the clouds. Nobody can disprove the miracle nor absolutely deny that Manuel, as Jurgen claims, had with tremendous rites redeemed his people from their sins, including nocturnal truancy. Upon Jurgen, unlikely rock, is reared a towering legend. Niafer chooses to remember her husband for his gentleness and purity and loving kindness, though his nine companions in the order of the Silver Stallion have no recollection of such qualities in Manuel. Holy Holmendis from Philistia, Niafer's spiritual adviser, sustains and even directs her in her choice of memories. Together the woman and the priest re-make, in the image of her jealous heart and his scheming head, the figure of Manuel, and with the cult of the Redeemer counsel, cajole, shame, and hammer Poictesme into virtue. In the end the hero that Manuel never was has civilized his violent realm, which cherishes him as a pattern of excellence and believes that he will come again in rewarding glory.

Ironically, poetically Mr. Cabell summarizes in his story of the remembered Manuel the histories of all redemptions. Those realists who had known the man as flesh and blood, hardy, cunning, terrible, yield in different fashions to the legend of the Redeemer "whom Gonfal repudiated as blown dust, and Miramon, as an impostor, and whom Coth repudiated out of honest love: but whom Guivric accepted, through two sorts of policy; whom Kerin accepted as an honorable old human foible, and Ninzian, as a pathetic and serviceable joke; whom Donander accepted wholeheartedly (to the eternal joy of Donander); and who was accepted also by Niafer, and by Jurgen the pawnbroker, after some little private reservations." The legend engulfs them all, and all their various stories. Mr. Cabell, as worldly as any who wondered at what memory had done to Manuel, points out with sly astuteness the interest and policy which help the myth along. But craft, in his record, only plants the seed and watches it. What makes the legend grow to messianic eminence is the eager soil it finds in the passion of the human race to forget the past and overlook the present in a blind aspiring. Manuel may have been barely great enough to hang a hope on. He survives because men desire him to, and, surviving, he becomes for them what they have shaped from the rude original. After they have dreamed him, they rise toward the level of their own dreams. Manuel, the splendid father of his county, is its still more splendid son. And Mr. Cabell, ironist of redemption, is no less its poet. If, with his tacit parallels, he suggests that other redeemers owe a good deal to men, he explicitly contends that men cannot do without redeemers. Over whatever prose poetry has power.

Manuel leaves, of course, actual children. Melicent, for instance, reappears as the radiant heroine of *Domnei*, loved by Perion de la Forêt. Partly because *Domnei*, originally called *The Soul of Melicent*, belongs to the period which produced *Chivalry*, and partly because it pretends to be a prose redaction of *Le Roman de Lusignan* by Nicolas de Caen, that invented poet, it has but few touches of bitter irony. It is Mr. Cabell's highest flight in the representation of the extravagant woman-worship developed out of the chivalric code—the worship which began by ascribing to the beloved the qualities of purity and perfection, of beauty and holiness, and ended by virtually identifying her with the divine. This high-flying folly can go no further than it goes in the careers of Perion and Melicent, who are so uplifted by ineffable desire that their souls reach ceaselessly out to each other though obstacles large as continents intervene. For Perion the most deadly battles are but thornpricks in the quest

of Melicent; and such is Melicent's loyalty that the possession of her body by Demetrios of Anatolia leaves her soul immaculate and almost unperturbed. In this tale love is canonized: throned on alabaster above all the vulgar gods it diffuses among its worshipers a crystal radiance in which mortal imperfections perish, or are at least forgotten during rapturous hours.

A cynical rogue like Jurgen might point out that Perion and Melicent have as an asset to their fidelity the advantage that they never meet during their long quest and might insinuate that they are simple creatures who run no risk of any withering contact with the intelligence. Nothing, in any case, pulls them down. Even that second of disappointment which Perion feels when Melicent comes to him in the bloody Court of Stars proves to be but one pulse-beat lost between his old loyalty and its more glorious successor. A consequence of such single-mindedness is that *Domnei* is unified and dramatic beyond any other of the Cabell novels. It lacks all the hocus-pocus of mythology; it is innocent of symbolism. Melicent and Perion have divided one idea between them, and they cherish the matched halves, as village lovers divide and cherish a sixpence. When Perion, taken prisoner by Demetrios, is threatened with his tortures, Melicent ransoms him with herself given in marriage to the proconsul; and when Melicent, in turn, is threatened with similar agonies, Perion buys the life of Demetrios at a great price and sends him back to her white arms. Their love is so powerful that it infects their world. Demetrios, who cannot understand it, is yet shamed by it. He withholds his greedy hands from Melicent and becomes the honorable rival of Perion. Even Ahasuerus the Jew, after his long scheming has made him master of the Melicent whom he has from the first desired, renounces her, contenting himself with the poor consolation that he, like Demetrios, surpasses Perion in his recognition of the true soul of Melicent. Are these actions merely gestures? Perhaps, but they are never empty. One by one they build up the illusion of a universe wherein love fulfills its blazing promises, out of the reach of fickleness or jealousy or the mere hunger of the senses. And with what steadiness Mr. Cabell unrolls his plot, proceeding from gesture to gesture till all his characters have been purged of their low motives and the lovers stand exultant in the noon of their victory over all unworthiness. With this intentness and steadiness of his conception goes the style of *Domnei*, which is lucid and unvaryingly lovely.

Connected remotely with the Jurgen saga is *The High Place*, which in lucidity if not in loveliness may be compared with *Domnei*. There is the minor connection that Florian de Puysange has the unlawful blood of Jurgen in him, and the major connection that that blood leads Florian along paths, as far away as the eighteenth century, which dimly recall the paths of Jurgen. For Florian is no single-hearted Perion de la Forêt, struggling forever up one mount of ecstasy. Almost at the beginning of the story he attains the Sleeping Beauty in the Wood, Melior, and is thereafter terribly bored by her; the four wives he has had already have not taught him to rise superior to disillusion. Nor is boredom his only fate; he is hoodwinked by her too, and deprived of all his grounds of faith. He who had won her cynically enough, making a pact with Janicot that she was to remain Florian's wife but a year and that Janicot was to have her child for his fee, finds that the child is not his own but Holy Hoprig's. Melior is a minx, and Hoprig, whom Poictesme has thought a saint, is a fraud. Beauty and holiness, that is to say, have connived to cheat Florian. This later Jurgen comes then to something like the conclusions of his legendary ancestor, and listens without too angry a dissent to the doctrine of worldly prudence as enunciated by his father: "To submit is the great lesson. I too was once a dreamer: and in dreams there are lessons. But to submit, without dreaming any more, is the great lesson; to submit, without either understanding or repining, and without demanding of life too much of beauty or of holiness, and without shirking the fact that this universe is under no least bond ever to grant us, upon either side of the grave, our desires. To do that, my son, does not satisfy and probably will not ever satisfy a Puysange. But to do that is wisdom."

Listening without too absolute a consent, for Florian is a Puysange, he yet agrees that in practice the one rule to follow is: "Thou shalt not offend against the notions of thy neighbor." Florian does not so offend, though he commits, in one way or another, almost all the other offenses possible. True, Mr. Cabell in the end explains that the whole story has been a dream of Florian's, brought on by his reading of Perrault's version of the Sleeping Beauty. It is, however, such a dream as would come to a Puysange, with the strain of Jurgen in him. *The High Place* is as diabolistic as *Domnei* is devout. The center of neither action lies within the confines of ordinary humanity. Florian is jauntily at ease with Janicot. And it is Janicot, the ancient adversary, who, talking with Michael the archangel, pronounces the commentary and the benediction: "I have never been omnipotent, I am not worshipped in any shining temple even to-day; but always I have been served. . . . God after god has set rules to bridle and to change the nature of my people. Meanwhile I do not meddle with their natures, I urge them to live in concord with their natures, and to make the most of my kingdom. . . . Your master is strong, as yet, and I too am strong, but neither of us is strong enough to control men's dreams. Now, the dreaming of men—mark you, I do not say of humankind, for women are rational creatures,—has an aspiring which is ruthless. It goes beyond decency, it aspires to more of perfectibility than any god has yet been able to provide or even to live up to. So this quite insane aspiring first sets up beautiful and holy gods in heaven, then in the dock; and, judging all by human logic, decrees this god not to be good enough. . . . It follows that all gods imaginable by men must always fall away into defeat and exile, because of men's implacable dreaming about more than men can imagine. It follows, too, that I go rather quietly about my kingdom, on account of my poor people's insane and toplofty dreaming."

Thus Janicot furnishes a key to Poictesme: it is a country in which men, fettered as they may be by space and time, by good and evil, dream triumphantly beyond them.

III. SCHOLIA

THOUGH Mr. Cabell has carried out to his own conclusion the most complete scheme of romance ever undertaken by an American romancer, he has met with strange fortunes on his devoted road. At the outset he seemed to slip into a prevailing category, and indeed seems almost to have put on as a disguise the cloak and sword of the prevailing fashion in romance. He prospered then, only, with the passing of the fashion, to fall into a decline of reputation not at all matched by any falling off in the quality of his product. From such a state he was rescued by the turmoil of eminence which followed the attacks upon *Jurgen*. This must have been as annoying to him as it was unjust to his masterpiece; it nevertheless enabled him to consolidate his position and to bring all his books back into circulation, revised to fit his matured scheme. Having stood since that episode in the rank of the later classics, he now perhaps runs the risk of being estimated by the hearsay which everybody knows without being studied by anybody with the care which he requires and deserves. His individual books may be delightful, but they revolve around the central sun of an idea without which he cannot be seen as entirely himself.

Late as he was in making his dominant idea explicit, he has made it thoroughly explicit in a series of commentaries which he calls Scholia and in the arrangement of his separate works in the eighteen volumes devoted to the Biography of Manuel. Certain of the Scholia, such as *The Judging of Jurgen* and *Taboo*, are minor answers to minor critics; *Joseph Hergesheimer* and *Some of Us*, while incidentally revealing, are chiefly his analyses of other writers. *The White Robe*, *The Way of Ecben*, and *The Music from Behind the Moon* are three chapters of what was to have been a whole book called *The Witch-Woman*. *The Lineage of Lichfield* is more significant. In it Mr. Cabell has painstakingly worked out the genealogy which furnishes the skeleton of his romantic scheme, tracing the ancestry of all his characters back along one line or other to the epic Manuel.

At the same time, he has confirmed these relationships by annotations, in the revised edition, to various of his stories which theretofore had seemed to stand alone. The genealogical unity of his imagined world, however, is but a symbol, chosen as a device of art to represent a truth of life. He himself has so well set forth his scheme in the Epistle Dedicatory to the *Lineage* that quotation is the best comment.

"Now on the face of it, as I have confessed, the thing is a pedigree which indicates the de scent of various persons, about whom I have written the stories and books named marginally, from Dom Manuel of Poictesme. In reality, I think, this volume is an outline—or, say, a map—of some nine centuries of Dom Manuel's life, the life of which my other books are the Biography. For, be it repeated, the life that informed tall Manuel the Redeemer did not become extinct when the old champion rode westward with Grandfather Death. The body and the appearance of Dom Manuel had gone. But his life remained perpetuated in divers children—in, to be accurate, a respectable total of sixteen persons,—who afterward transmitted this life to their progeny, as did they in turn to their own offspring. So this life flowed on through time,—and through such happenings in France and England and America as, one by one, my books have recorded,—with every generation dividing and subdividing the troubled and attritioned flowing into more numerous streamlets. . . .

"It is about this life that I have written elsewhere, in many places, in various chapters of a Biography which is largish now, but stays incomplete, and may not ever be completed. For this human life, as I write about it, appears to me a stream that, in journeying toward an unpredictable river, itself the tributary of an unplumbed ocean, is fretted equally (still to preserve the fluvial analogue) by the winds of time and by many pebbles of chance. So are there various ripples raised upon the stream as it goes—ultimately—seaward: and, noting these, we say this ripple is Manuel, that Ormskirk, and the other Charteris; noting also that while we name it the small stir is gone. But the stream remains unabated, nor is the sureness of its moving lessened, any more than is the obscurity of its goal.

"Or let us shift the figure. Let us rather liken this continuously reincarnated life of Manuel to an itinerant comedian that with each generation assumes the garb of a new body, and upon a new stage enacts a variant of yesterday's drama. For I do not find the comedy ever to be much altered in its essentials. . . . The first act is the imagining of the place where contentment exists and may be come to; and the second act reveals the striving toward, and the third act the falling short of, that shining goal, or else (the difference here being negligible) the attaining of it, to discover that happiness, after all, abides a thought farther down the bogged, rocky, clogged, befogged heart-breaking road, if anywhere. That is the comedy which, to my finding, . . . the life I write about has enacted over and over again on every stage between Poictesme and Lichfield.

"I call it a comedy. Really there is thin sustenance for the tragic muse in the fact that with each performance the costume of the protagonist is spoiled, and the human body temporarily informed with Manuel's life is thrown perforce to the dust-heap. There is not even apparent, to reflection, any economic loss: for the wardrobe of this mundivagant posturer is self-replenishing, in that as each costume is used it thriftily begets new apparel for the comedian to ruin in to-morrow's rendering of the old play. The parent's flesh is flung by like an outworn coat: but the comedian, reclad with the child's body, tricked out with strong fresh sinews and re-rouged with youth, is lustily refurbishing, with a garnish of local allusions and of the latest social and religious and political slang, all yesterday's archaic dialogue and inveterate 'situations.'"

Mr. Cabell understands that formerly, "they whisper, the scenery was arboreal, and our comedian wore fur and a tail; as before that his costume was reptilian, and yet earlier was piscine. So do the scientists trace backward his career to life's first appearance upon the stage, when the *vis comica* which later was to animate the thews of Manuel had for its modest apparel only a small single bubble embedded in primeval slime." And, since "our comedian has dressed his rôle with increasing elaborateness, progressing from a mere pinhead of sentiency to all the intricate fripperies of the human body," Mr. Cabell likewise understands that "to-morrow the age-old comedian will be doing and wearing none knows what, although in reason the restless artist that we call life cannot long stay content with human bodies for his apparel and medium. Already, in considerate eyes, life tends to some more handsome expression, by means of the harnessed chemistries and explosions, and collaborating flywheels and vapors, and wire-dancing thunderbolts, that in all our cities dwarf the human beings who serve as the release levers." Still, history is vague and prophecy is futile, so Mr. Cabell limits his Biography to the materials which he can examine. "I merely know that, even though the life of our planet may by and by discard mankind just as it has discarded the dodo and the dinosaur, at present men and women are life's clothing: and I take it to be the part of urbanity to accept the mode of our day."

The march of the Biography has at last, thanks to the *Lineage* and to the collected edition of Mr. Cabell's *Works*, become traceable. Starting out with *Figures of Earth: A Comedy of Appearances*, it introduces Manuel and Poictesme with something of the geography and mythology of the province. *The Silver Stallion: A Comedy of Redemption* deals next with the posthumous Manuel. Then follow the tales in the line of chivalry, *Domnei; The Music from Behind the Moon: Two Comedies of Woman-Worship* and *Chivalry: Dizain des Reines*. Returning along its chronological path, the Biography studies the career of Manuel's great contemporary in *Jurgen: A Comedy of Justice*, and from it proceeds, by what may be called the line of gallantry, through *The Line of Love: Dizain des Mariages, The High Place: A Comedy of Disenchantment*, and *Gallantry: Dizain des Fêtes Galantes*, to the middle of the eighteenth century. Turning back once more, the Biography brings up the line of poetry in *Something About Eve: A Comedy of Fig-Leaves, The Certain Hour: Dizain des Poëtes, The Cords of Vanity: A Comedy of Shirking*, to Mr. Cabell's own verses and one formal comedy, *From the Hidden Way; The Jewel Merchants: Dizain and Comedy of Echoes*. Finally come the other novels with an American setting, *The Rivet in Grandfather's Neck: A Comedy of Limita-*

tions, *The Eagle's Shadow: A Comedy of Purse-Strings*, and *The Cream of the Jest: A Comedy of Evasions*, the last of which, by exhibiting the double life of its hero in Poictesme and in Lichfield, brings the two ends of the Biography together, where they are bound with the *Lineage of Lichfield*. The end of the Biography is reached in *Townsend of Lichfield: Dizain des Adieux*, which gathers up the various Scholia and says farewell. There remain to be listed only the prologue, *Beyond Life: Dizain des Dèmiurges*, and the epilogue, *Straws and Prayer-Books: Dizain des Diversions*.

Mr. Cabell includes his prologue and epilogue in the Biography, but they may also be considered among the Scholia. Roughly speaking, the first explains what he makes of the universe, and the second why he has made his books. In the universe, at least so far as it concerns itself with men and women, he finds that the one non-negligible element is romance, "the first and loveliest daughter of human vanity," by which mankind is deceived, itself eagerly taking part in the deception, and is thereby exalted. "No one upon the preferable side of Bedlam wishes to be reminded of what we are in actuality, even were it possible, by any disastrous miracle, ever to dispel the mist which romance has evoked about all human beings." For the estate of man upon his planet is trifling. "All about us flows and gyrates unceasingly the material universe," Mr. Cabell makes John Charteris say, in *Beyond Life*, "an endless inconceivable jumble of rotatory blazing gas and frozen spheres and detonating comets, wherethrough spins Earth like a frail midge. And to this blown molecule adhere what millions and millions and millions of parasites just such as I am, begetting and dreaming and slaying and abnegating and toiling and making mirth, just as did aforetime those countless generations of our forebears, every one of whom was likewise a creature just such as I am! . . . And still—behold the miracle!—still I believe life to be a personal transaction between myself and Omnipotence; I believe that what I do is somehow of importance; and I believe that I am on a journey toward some very public triumph not unlike that of the third prince in the fairy-tale." Only with the help of this persistent self-delusion has the race been able to endure its plight.

So the first man tricked himself into the devout belief that the naked apes must triumph over all their rivals in the struggle for hegemony; so the last man will continue to play ape to his dreams. Romance, then, which begets these dynamic illusions, is a demiurge, a force poured into the stream of life so near its source that it may no longer be separated from the stream, and certainly may not be disregarded by any of the stream's historians.

As aspects of romance, as creations of the demiurge, Mr. Cabell studies the principal motives which direct the human enterprise. There is chivalry, a notion founded upon no ascertainable testimony, to the effect that men are not only the favored children of the gods but are their representatives in a foreign country, and so are obliged to bear themselves as much like gods as may be. Sustained by this conception, what pinnacles of self-reliant virtue have not men aspired to, and sometimes reached! There is love, which, springing from a fierce animal desire, has been now narrowed and now enlarged until it embraces consideration and reverence and a sensibility so acute as occasionally to disavow the original impulse.

"When you come to judge," says Charteris, what man has made of the raw materials of love, "appraising the deed in view as against the wondrous overture of courtship and that infinity of high achievements which time has seen performed as grace-notes, words fail before his egregious thaumaturgy." There is common-sense, "another dynamic illusion, through which romance retains the person of average intelligence in physical employment and, as a by-product, in an augmenting continuance of creature comforts," as if prudence were more than an affair of the swift moment and as if the things called practical had any ultimate value in the whirling current of existence. There is religion, based upon the primitive suspicion which men had that the seen activities of nature must be manipulated by unseen beings, extended to the hope that these unseen beings were vitally interested in mankind, and raised finally to the confidence that there was another universe in which men would be rewarded or punished for their doings and thoughts in this one. "And religion, like all the other products of romance, is true in a far higher sense than are the unstable conditions of our physical life. Indeed, the most prosaic of materialists proclaim that we are all descended from an insane fish, who somehow evolved the idea that it was his duty to live on land, and eventually succeeded in doing it. So, now that his earth-treading progeny manifest the same illogical aspiration toward heaven, their bankruptcy in common-sense may, even by material standards, have much the same incredible result."

Nor in the secular spheres are the motives of mankind less clearly the illusions of romance. Art but seduces the artist, at almost every personal cost to himself, into the assurance that he can catch beauty or truth in the net of his own vision and so transmit something eternal to posterity, when as a matter of fact posterity will perhaps not even notice him and certainly will not long bear him in mind as anything more noticeable than a classic. Patriotism, too, is an anodyne which the demiurge administers to save men from the bewilderment and panic they would possibly feel if they once admitted that they live in nations governed by other men not essentially wiser than themselves, an anodyne which drugs them into national complacency or lifts them to a burning loyalty to what they hold to be the national good. And as to optimism, what could be more unwarrantable an illusion, among the fortuitous items of experience, than the creed which promises that any given chain of events must have the happy ending found nowhere in the universe except in second-rate romances? In short, the demiurge of romance is the element in life which rounds out with curves and colors the clumsily articulated skeleton of fact, thereby serving, with the truest utility which may be asked of it, to add to the dull condition of the brutes the human desiderata of distinction and clarity, and beauty and symmetry, and tenderness and truth and urbanity.

That Mr. Cabell does not condemn all these illusions is evidenced by the labor he has put into his Biography. "From the beginning," says John Charteris with his author's approbation, "I have been contending that nothing in the universe is of importance, or is authentic to any serious sense, except the various illusions of romance, the demiurge." No Biographer with any gift of irony could have persisted, through all the work which makes up the eighteen volumes, in the chronicling of mere painted mirages. *Straws and Prayer-Books*, the explanatory epilogue, inventories and anatomizes the motives which, so far as Mr. Cabell is aware of them, have impelled him to the long task. His motives really come down to one. "The artist," he commences, "or, at least, the artist who happens to be a novelist, —is life's half-frightened playboy." As other men devise for themselves the fictions by which they live, he devises fictions for himself and them, constructing in the process certain pleasant imaginative alcoves in which all who will may linger as they advance toward death "through gray and monotonous corridors." The artist, however, must not be tricked, as Mr. Cabell says he has not been, into "the deadly error of succumbing to praiseworthy motives" and thus "misled into evanescence through philanthropy . . . For the one really ponderable sort of writer—the writer who communicates to us something of his own delight and interest in his playing, and who thus in the end contributes to our general human happiness,—has been influenced while about this playing by none save selfish considerations. He has written wholly to divert himself: he has for that moment been inclavated to pleasure-seeking with somewhat the ruthlessness of a Nero and all the tenacity of a débutante: and if I seem unduly to emphasize this obvious fact, it is merely because the man afterward so often lies about it."

Most thoroughly to divert himself, says Mr. Cabell, avoiding the dangerous first person by speaking in the third, the artist makes sport with the three martinets which he, like other men at bottom, genuinely abhors: common-sense and piety and death. "The literary artist . . . temporarily endows his followers with the illusion of possessing what all alchemists have sought—unfading youth, wealth and eternal life. He engineers the escape for which men have always longed, and which they have always known to be attainable, as here, by magic." So Mr. Cabell has left behind the flat terrain of common-sense and has laid the scene of his actions within or somewhere near the magical boundaries of Poictesme. Moreover: "Everywhere through the shadowland of legend canter and gallop—with the gleaming eyes of nocturnal creatures, with a multitudinous tossed shining of steel,—these 'squires of the night's body, Diana's foresters, these minions of the moon,' whom the prosaic call thieves and highwaymen: and everywhere men have admired and cherished some cunning, strong, unconquerable rogue." And the artist also, set by his profession a little outside of the sleek and ordered universe, has given his allegiance less to the established gods than to Pan, the scapegoat of nature, the outcast god "who had looked upon the divine handiwork, and seen that it was not good; or, at any rate, not good enough." So Mr. Cabell has left to others the austere task of penning the lives of the saints and has himself created Jurgen and his experimental crew. Above all, men have abhorred death, a thing so dreadful to them that except in special instances they prefer to it the twin tediums of common-sense and piety. "None the less, it is with this omnipresent and omnicorporeal monarch that the artist makes sport, depriving death of terrors with the opiates of religion: and maiming death of potency likewise, so long as the artist eludes destruction and survives in his art." So Mr. Cabell, aware of the impending ugliness as only the lover of loveliness can be, for twenty-five years toilsomely kept on piling his bright pebbles upon his shining cairn in honor of Manuel.

Yet what, he says he asked himself just before ending his explanation, has he got out of his work on the Biography? His first answer was that he had got nothing, since "the outcome of his multifold playing . . . was always unpredictable, always chance-guided, and, in any case, was of no benefit or hurt to him by and by, and was never of any grave importance to anybody else." But on further thought he found a second answer to his question. "I really had got out of life what I most wanted. I had wanted to make the Biography . . . and I had made it, in just the way which it seemed good to me. To do that had been, no doubt, my play and my diversion, in the corridors where men must find diversion . . . or else go mad. . . . But . . . it seemed to me, too, that I had somehow fulfilled, without unduly shirking, an obligation which had been laid upon me to make the Biography. I was not, heaven knew, claiming for myself any heavenly inspiration or even any heavenly countenance. Rather, it seemed to me that the ability and the body and the life which transiently were at my disposal had been really used: with these lent implements which were not ever properly speaking mine, and which presently would be taken away from me, I had made something which was actually mine. . . . Here then, upon this shelf, in these green volumes which contain the entire Life of Manuel in its final form, I can lay hand and eye upon just what precisely my life has amounted to: the upshot of my existence is here before me, a tangible and visible and entirely complete summing up, within humiliatingly few inches. And yet, as I consider these inadequate green volumes, I suspect that the word I am looking for is 'gratitude.'"

In this conclusion, which only by the shorter-sighted codes of philanthropy can be adjudged arrogant, Mr. Cabell has modestly kept faith with his whole creed. Looking back over the course of the Biography he suspects that he has played in it the rôle of Horvendile, "the erratic demiurge who composes and controls the entire business extempore, without any prompter except his own æsthetic whims."

He reasons that it must have been vain, but he testifies that it has been pleasant. It remains for others, susceptible or not to Mr. Cabell's reasoning in the matter, to bear witness to the general pleasure which has been the by-product of his private diversion.

Those others, however susceptible, will not linger too long over his reasoning about the vast futility of human life. This is an ancient doctrine, shared by all who keep their eyes wide open as they charge the impregnable walls of fate. Nor will those other men for whom Mr. Cabell has incidentally constructed his charming alcoves linger too long over the central conception about which the Biography has been arranged. Ingenious and arresting as it is, it insists upon recalling certain words of its originator to the effect that "it is the nature of every explanatory theory to be evolved after the phenomena it accounts for." The author of the Biography must be estimated, like any other artist, by his actual performances; theories are for critics. If he gives delight by his bold playing with ideas, he gives still more by the energy, never imitable in mere discourse, with which he puts such ideas into action in the behavior of the characters he has created. More beguilingly than did ever Solon or Lycurgus, Mr. Cabell has outlined the polity of Poictesme; like another Manuel, he has robustly peopled it, endowing it, possibly, with as long a life as some identifiable medieval counties had. His people have, if not the dimensions of verisimilitude, the unmistakableness of visions; bull-necked Manuel, eating his proud heart amid the tumult of affairs; the nine lords of the Fellowship of the Silver Stallion, genial murderers and ruthless lovers; lank Jurgen, considering the universe with a mind as free and nimble as the recalcitrant Pan's; Melicent and Perion, blown over seas and mountains in their disunited flesh, but in their spirits forever clasped in one undying rapture; the lords of Puysange, supple and insolent in the face of whatever adventures; gallant, hardy, disillusioned Ormskirk, master of brave gestures and difficult occasions; John Charteris, airy commentator in a world through which he flounders; besides these, scores of slighter heroes, cut no doubt by the pattern of Manuel, but perennially re-enacting the unavoidable comedy with delicate variations; and besides all these, the exquisite glimmering girls, the radiant women, who are the ends of the heroes' pursuits and the enrichments and torments of their successes. A philosopher might have incubated the theory upon which the Biography is based; a critic might have elaborated the scheme of carrying Manuel through many metempsychoses; only a poet, authentically gifted, could have created the figures which now inhabit Poictesme.

Mr. Cabell is not, however, at his most poetical in his verse. *From the Hidden Way* belongs, in a sense, with the Scholia, being made up in considerable part of what pretend to be English adaptations of originals by Alessandro de Medici, Raimbaut de Vaqueiras, Nicholas de Caen, Antoine Riczi, Charles Garnier, Théodore Passerat, Alphonse Moreau, and Paul Verville—some of them imaginary and some of them characters of the Biography, where poems by them also appear. The pretended adaptations are occasionally fresh and sweet; the sonnets, especially, wherein Mr. Cabell speaks in his own person, have a convincing timbre; but as a whole his poems give the impression of being first drafts or subsequent paraphrases of passages better rendered in the prose. He has very rarely, when working with rhyme and meter, quite fitted his matter to his own natural rhythm, which is a prose rhythm, delicate, balanced, and idiosyncratic beyond the reach of most regular verse. A single comparison is enough. He has never been happier as a poet than in the lines, ascribed to Alessandro de Medici, which bear the title, *But Wisdom Is Justified of Her Children:*

"Phyllida, spring wakes about us—
Wakes to mock at us and flout us
That so coldly do delay:
When the very birds are mating,
Pray you, why should we be waiting—
We that might be wed to-day?

"*Life is brief*, the wise men tell us;—
Even those dusty, musty fellows
That have done with life,—and pass
Where the wraith of Aristotle
Hankers, vainly, for a bottle,
Youth and some frank Grecian lass.

"Ah, I warrant you;—and Zeno
Would not reason, now, could he know
One more chance to live and love:
For, at best, the merry May-time
Is a very fleeting playtime;—
Why, then, waste an hour thereof?

"Plato, Solon, Periander,
Seneca, Anaximander,
Pyrrho, and Parmenides!
Were one hour alone remaining
Would ye spend it in attaining
Learning, or to lips like these?

"Thus, I demonstrate by reason
Now is our predestined season
For the garnering of all bliss;
Prudence is but long-faced folly;
Cry a fig for melancholy!
Seal the bargain with a kiss."

Deft and spirited as these lines are, they strike the ear with the accents of another century, a little thin, a little derivative. With how much more substance, with how much richer and deeper rhythms Horvendile in *The Cream of the Jest* is allowed to apostrophize Ettarre, speaking perfectly of beautiful old happenings in the language of a new rapture!

"Assuredly, it was you of whom blind Homer dreamed, comforting endless night with visions of your beauty, as you sat in a bright fragrant vaulted chamber weaving at a mighty loom, and embroidering on tapestry the battles men were waging about Troy because of your beauty; and very certainly it was to you that Hermes came over fields of violets and parsley, where you sang magic rhymes, sheltered by an island cavern, in which cedar and citron-wood were burning—and, calling you Calypso, bade you release Odysseus from the spell of your beauty. Sophocles, too, saw you bearing an ewer of bronze, and treading gingerly among gashed lamentable corpses, lest your loved dead be dishonored; and Sophocles called you Antigone, praising your valor and your beauty. And when men named you Bombyca, Theocritus also sang of your grave drowsy voice and your feet carven of ivory, and of your tender heart and all your honey-pale sweet beauty. . . .

"And as Mark's Queen, . . . you strayed with Tristran in the sunlit glades of Morois, that high forest, where many birds sang full-throated in the new light of spring; as Medeia you fled from Colchis; and as Esclairmonde you delivered Huon from the sardonic close wiles of heathenry, which to you seemed childish. All poets have had these fitful glimpses of you, Ettarre, and of that perfect beauty which is full of troubling reticences, and so, is somehow touched with something sinister.

Now all these things I likewise see in you, Ettarre; and therefore, for my own sanity's sake, I dare not concede that you are a human being."

At such moments the poet in Mr. Cabell takes him well beyond the reach of the Scholiast in him. Other scholiasts, however, may still be drawn to the task of dealing with the critical problems he presents. One problem, in particular, invites: the problem as to what place he occupies in the literature of his native country.

There seems to be no longer any reason for not associating him with the only comparable American romancers, Hawthorne and Melville. Unlike the others as each of these three may seem, they have all at least this much in common, that they are engineers of escape from the universe of compromises and half-measures to the universe in which both the reason and the imagination would prefer to live. Hawthorne was indeed more strictly bound to the actual world than either of the others, yet he too breathed uncomfortably in it, and kept sending his imagination back to times in which it could function without the daily handicaps which fretted him. Only in the dim world of old Salem could he imagine the proud spirit of Hester Prynne rising up and cracking the stiff frame of the Puritan code. Melville, less touched by Puritanism than Hawthorne, fled from his world not along the track of time but along the track of space, sending his imagination to a cannibal paradise in the Pacific, to the wild frontiers of the remote ocean where his countrymen wrestled with angels and demons. Mr. Cabell, more systematic than Melville or Hawthorne in his thinking, is more thorough in his art. He has left behind both his own place and his own age, and has taken refuge in an imagined realm where the very shadows are brighter than the sunshine of Virginia. He pays for this greater detachment with a certain rarefaction; Hawthorne is more solid, Melville more robust. It is in wit and loveliness that Mr. Cabell matches them.

Melville, to be sure, is one of the wittiest of romancers. But he never won for his wit a full emancipation from the fears which had been planted in him by his moral training. He fought with the beasts of conscience; he tortured himself with speculations about immortality; he could carry even Captain Ahab only as far as to the sulphurous brink of blasphemy. With conscience and immortality and blasphemy Mr. Cabell's wit plays as intrepidly as with less formidable prejudices. It has no fears. It stares open-eyed at the blazing sun and good-humoredly strokes the beard of Jehovah. There is, consequently, none of that violence which goes with Melville's robuster and racier comedy. So are there in Mr. Cabell none of the touches of provincialism which go with Hawthorne's solider grasp of human character. Is Donatello a faun? Jurgen is, too. But whereas in the substantial tissue of Donatello the sense of sin takes root, Jurgen slips through earth and heaven and hell as unassailably as if Luther had never lived to make men forever conscious of the moral bearing of all things. Mr. Cabell is thus as free to admire loveliness wherever he finds it as to discover the possibilities of mirth in whatever theme. He finds beauty glittering in the midst of ugly sins, and snares it in his tolerant net. He builds fresh beauty about ominous symbols, inventing or elaborating them if need be. He does not, like Hawthorne, feel the obligation constantly to check the wings of his vision by comparing it with reality. Mr. Cabell, by questioning the reality of reality, has been naturalized in the world of dreams till he moves about there without the scruples lasting over from another allegiance. Thus the beauty of his Poictesme is double-distilled. Those lovers of beauty who must now and then come down to earth for renewal will occasionally gasp in Poictesme, wishing the atmosphere would thicken and the brilliant colors change. But always Poictesme hangs above the mortal clouds, suspended from the eternal sky, in the region where wit and beauty are joined in an everlasting kiss.

THE BOOKS OF JAMES BRANCH CABELL

Listed in the order in which they have been finally arranged in the Storisende Edition of The Works of James Branch Cabell, 18 vols., 1927–1930, published by Robert M. McBride, by whom the books are issued also in separate form, as below:

BIOGRAPHY

1. Beyond Life: Dizain des Démiurges. 1919.
2. Figures of Earth: A Comedy of Appearances. 1921.
3. The Silver Stallion: A Comedy of Redemption. 1926.
4. Domnei: A Comedy of Woman-Worship. Revised edition with an introduction by Joseph Hergesheimer. 1920. (Originally published as The Soul of Melicent in 1913.)
5. Chivalry: Dizain des Reines. Revised edition with an introduction by Burton Rascoe. 1921. (Originally published in 1909.)
6. Jurgen: A Comedy of Justice. 1919.
7. The Line of Love: Dizain des Mariages. Revised edition with an introduction by H. L. Mencken. 1921. (Originally published in 1905.)
8. The High Place: A Comedy of Disenchantment. 1923.
9. Gallantry: Dizain des Fêtes Galantes. Revised edition with an introduction by Louis Untermeyer. 1922. (Originally published in 1907.)

10. Something About Eve: A Comedy of Fig-Leaves. 1927.
11. The Certain Hour: Dizain des Poëtes. 1916.
12. The Cords of Vanity: A Comedy of Shirking. Revised edition with an introduction by Wilson Follett. 1920. (Originally published in 1909.)
13. From the Hidden Way: Dizain des Échos. Revised edition. 1924. (Originally published in 1916.)
14. The Rivet in Grandfather's Neck: A Comedy of Limitations. 1915.
15. The Eagle's Shadow: A Comedy of Purse-Strings. Revised edition with an introduction by Edwin Bjorkman. 1923. (Originally published in 1904.)
16. The Cream of the Jest: A Comedy of Evasions. Revised edition with an introduction by Harold Ward. 1922. (Originally published in 1917.)
17. Straws and Prayer-Books: Dizain des Diversions. 1924.
18. Townsend of Lichfield: Dizain des Adieux. 1930.

(The foregoing eighteen books have been further revised in the Storisende Edition and furnished with detailed and amusing Author's Notes.)

GENEALOGY

(All privately issued in Richmond, not by Robert M. McBride)

1. Branch of Abingdon. 1911.
2. Branchiana. 1907.
3. The Majors and Their Marriages. 1915.

SCHOLIA

(All issued by Robert M. McBride with the exceptions noted)

1. The Judging of Jurgen. 1920. (Originally published

in Chicago and incorporated the next year in the London edition of Jurgen, as in subsequent American editions.)

2. Taboo. 1921.
3. The Jewel Merchants. 1921. (Included in Vol. 13 of the Storisende Edition.)
4. Joseph Hergesheimer. 1921. (Originally published in Chicago and incorporated in Straws and Prayer-Books.)
5. The Lineage of Lichfield. 1922. (Included in Vol. 16 of the Storisende Edition.)
6. The Music from Behind the Moon. 1926. (Originally published by the John Day Company but included in Vol. 4 of the Storisende Edition.)
7. The White Robe. 1928. (Included in Vol. 18 of the Storisende Edition.)
8. The Way of Ecben. 1929. (Included in Vol. 18 of the Storisende Edition.)
9. Sonnets from Antan. 1930. (Originally published by the Fountain Press but included in Vol. 18 of the Storisende Edition.)
10. Some of Us: An Essay in Epitaphs. 1930.
11. These Restless Heads: A Trilogy of Romantics. 1932.

. . . .

Between Dawn and Sunrise. 1930. (A selection from Mr. Cabell's writings edited by John Macy.)